Christmas Day, 2003

Dearest Josie:

I think you live in the perfect place to know all about snow — and the snow goose! We hope this book will bring you many happy minutes (and hours) — of joy. With our love,

Grandma & Grandpa Davis

First published in the United States, Great Britain, Canada,
Australia, and New Zealand in 1993 by North-South Books,
an imprint of Nord-Süd Verlag AG, Gossau Zürich, Switzerland.

Distributed in the United States by North-South Books Inc., New York.

Library of Congress Cataloging-in-Publication Data is available.
ISBN 1-55858-194-4 (trade binding)
ISBN 1-55858-195-2 (library binding)

British Library Cataloguing in Publication Data
Vainio, Pirkko
Snow Goose
I. Title II. James, J. Alison
833.914
ISBN 1-55858-194-4

1 3 5 7 9 10 8 6 4 2
Printed in Belgium

The Snow Goose

by Pirkko Vainio

Translated by J. Alison James

North-South Books
New York

Once there was a girl named Anna who lived on a farm in a small town. The winters there were long and full of snow. Anna's grandfather lived nearby in an old farmhouse. In his stables, Grandfather kept a donkey, a pair of hens, and a multitude of cats.

One afternoon, when the winter was almost over, there was a fresh snowfall. Anna ran to the yard and began to build something out of the snow. The children next door came over and stayed to watch. "What are you making?" they called.

"A snow goose," Anna explained. Anna loved geese best of all. "She is sleeping now. And her head is tucked under her wing."

That night Anna had a lovely dream. She flew high over the snowy hills, clinging tightly to the snow goose. They flew over towns with glittering lights that looked like clouds of stars. How wonderful it was to fly!

When Anna woke up, she ran right to the window to check on her snow goose. But where was it? The snow goose was gone! Quickly Anna pulled on her boots and coat and ran outside.

The snow had all melted away. Anna stood right where she had built the snow goose, but there was nothing left! She went out to the field to search for it.

"If she has flown away . . . will she be able to find her way back here again?" Anna asked herself, and she flattened a little pile of snow with her feet.

Day by day it grew warmer. One day, when Anna was leaning on the garden gate, she saw Grandfather coming down the road with slow, heavy steps. He had something white in his arms.

Anna ran to him. "A snow goose!" she called.

"The goose is hurt. We have to take care of her," said Grandfather. His voice sounded strained.

Anna stared at the goose with wide eyes.

"Don't ask me where she came from or how she hurt herself," said Grandfather. "Because I don't know."

Anna felt her heart beat in her throat. My snow goose has come back, she thought.

Anna and Grandfather made a nest out of straw in the stable for the goose. Carefully Grandfather laid her down while Anna got water. Anna stayed in the stall the whole day. She sat quietly near the sleeping goose. She is very sick, thought Anna.

Occasionally the goose would wake up and move a little. Then Anna dripped some water on her beak. Anna was glad that she could take care of her.

The next morning Anna ran straight to the stable. Grandfather came right out.

"Anna," said Grandfather, looking at her gravely, "your goose is dead."

Anna stood in the door of the stall and her face grew hot. She turned abruptly and ran back to the house. The tears stormed over her cheeks.

It rained. Anna stared at the heavy raindrops running down the windowpanes. All of a sudden she saw Grandfather's wet face at the window. "Anna, come quickly. Your goose has left us something!"

Grandfather took Anna by the hand. The two of them ran across the barnyard.

In the middle of the goose's nest lay a great white egg. Grandfather had set a lamp over it to keep it warm.

"Will it live?" Anna asked, and she touched the egg carefully. It felt smooth and warm.

"If you take good care of it," said Grandfather.

Every day Anna went to the stall and turned the egg a little, so it would be warm on all sides.

Then one sunny morning Anna saw that the shell had a little crack in it. After a while a tiny beak peeked out, and shortly after, a little wet head—then the baby goose was hatched! The gosling turned itself under the warm lamp until it was dry, and then took its first uncertain steps over to Anna. "I will take good care of you," Anna whispered.

Summer came, with fresh, sunny days. Often it was windy, and the sky was a radiant blue.

Anna let the little goose out in the yard. With funny waddling steps it followed Anna everywhere. Every evening, Anna brought it back to the stable, and every morning the goose woke Anna up with a loud honk.

When it was really hot, Anna and the little goose went down to the pond. They paddled and splashed and had swimming races. Swimming, the little goose would always win. But when they ran back over the field, Anna would come in first.

After these outings Anna would sit under the great tree and the little goose would lay its head against Anna's neck.

Soon the little goose learned to fly.

One day when Anna was in the meadow, watching her goose fly overhead, a line of snow geese approached, honking. Anna's snow goose flew up to join them.

For a moment Anna thought her snow goose was looking back at her, but then the flock of geese circled higher and flew off, disappearing into the sky.

After her goose had been gone a few days, Anna asked her grandfather, "Do you think that she will come back?"

"Snow geese are wild creatures, Anna," said Grandfather, and he shook his head. "But who knows? . . ."